To access your free audio download, visit:

www.hmhbooks.com/freedownloads

Access code: CG50HOSPITAL

Curious George

Goes to the Hospital

by

Margret & H. A. Rey

HOUGHTON MIFFLIN HARCOURT

Boston New York

Originally published in collaboration with the
Children's Hospital Medical Center, Boston.

www.hmhco.com
www.curiousgeorge.com

Library of Congress Catalogue Control Number 65-19301

ISBN 978-0-544-76408-8
Manufactured in China
SCP 10 9 8 7 6 5 4 3 2 1
4500631845

This is George.

He lived with his friend, the man with the yellow hat. He was a good little monkey, but he was always curious.

Today George was curious about the big box on the man's desk.

What could be in it? George could not resist.
He simply HAD to open it.

It was full of funny little pieces of all sorts of
shapes and all sorts of colors.

George took one out.
It looked like a
piece of candy.

Maybe it WAS candy. Maybe he could eat it.
George put the piece in his mouth—and before
he knew it, he had swallowed it.

A while later the man with the yellow hat came home. "Why, George," he said, "I see you have already opened the box with the jigsaw puzzle. It was supposed to be a surprise for you. Well, let's go to work on it."

Finally the puzzle was finished—
well, almost finished.
One piece was missing.

The man looked for it everywhere, but he could not find it. "That's strange," he said, "it's a brand-new puzzle. Well, it cannot be helped. Maybe we'll find it in the morning. Let's go to bed now, George."

The next morning George did not feel well. He had a tummy-ache and did not want to eat his breakfast.

The man was worried. He went to the telephone and called Doctor Baker. "I'll be over as soon as I can," said the doctor.

First Doctor Baker looked down George's throat and felt his tummy. Then he took out his stethoscope and listened. "I'm not sure what's wrong," he said. "You'd better take George to the hospital and have an X-ray taken. I'll call them and let them know you are coming."

"Don't worry, George," said the man when they were driving to the hospital, "you have been there before, when you broke your leg. Remember how nice the doctors and nurses were?"

George held his big rubber ball tight as they walked up the hospital steps.

A nurse took them down a long hallway to a room where she gave George something to drink that looked white and tasted sweet. "It is called barium," the nurse explained. "It helps the doctors find out what is wrong with you, George."

In the next room stood a big table, and a doctor was just putting on a heavy apron. Then he

gave the man one just like it. George was curious: Would he get one too? No, he did not.

"You get on that table, George," the doctor said. "I am going to take some X-ray pictures of your insides." He pushed a button and there was a funny noise. "There—now you may get up, and we will have the X-rays developed right away."

"Now let's see . . . There is something there that should not be," said the doctor when they were looking at the X-rays.

"Why, that looks like . . . I think that must be the piece that was missing in our jigsaw puzzle yesterday!" said the man. "Well, well, well," said the doctor, "at least we know now what is wrong with our little patient. I'll tell Doctor Baker right away. George will have to stay at the hospital for a few days. They'll put a tube down his throat to get the piece out. It's only a small operation. I'll call a nurse and have her take you to the admitting office."

Many people were waiting outside the office. George had to wait too.

"Look, Betsy," the woman next to him said to her little girl, "there is Curious George!" Betsy looked up for a moment, but she did not even smile. Betsy had never been to a hospital before. She was scared.

15

Finally it was George's turn.

A pretty young nurse took him to the next room
—my, how many rooms and how many nurses
there were! One nurse wrote down a lot of things
about George: his name and his address and what
was wrong with him. Another nurse put a bracelet
around his wrist. "It has
your name on it, George,"
she said, "so that every-
body knows who you are."

Then the pretty young nurse came back. "My name is Carol," she said. "I am going to take you to your room now—we call it the children's ward —and put you to bed. There will be lots of children to keep you company."

And so it was. There were a lot of children in
the room. Some were up and around; others were
in their beds, with a doctor or a nurse looking
after them.

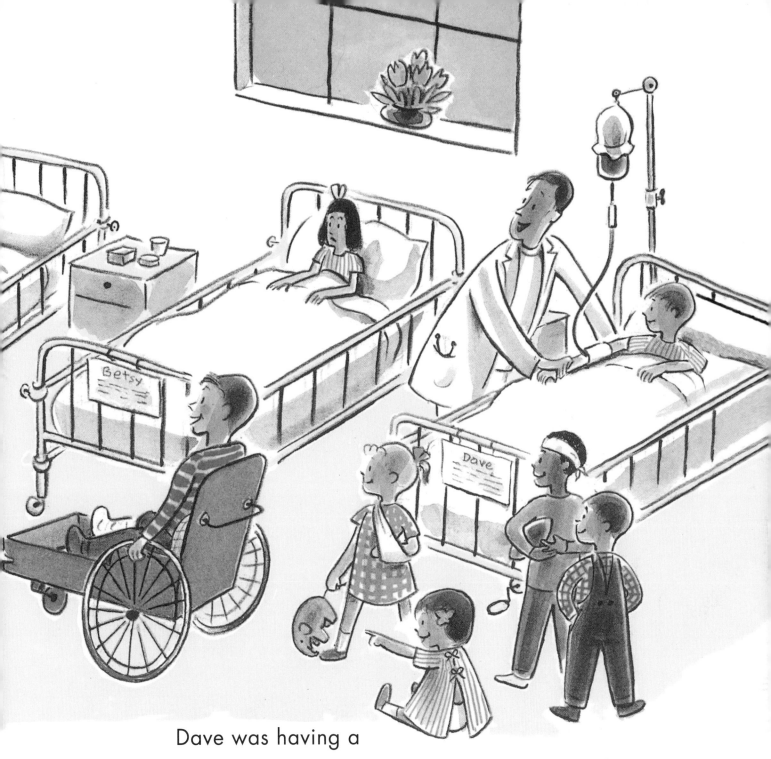

Dave was having a
blood transfusion. Steve had his leg bandaged
and was sitting in a go-cart. Betsy was in bed
looking sad. George got the bed next to Betsy.

19

George was glad when he
was in his bed at last. His tummy
was hurting again.

The man sat with him for a while. "Now I have
to leave you, George," he finally said. "I'll be
back first thing in the morning before they take you
to the operating room.
Nurse Carol will tuck
you in when it's time
to sleep."

Then he left. George
just sat there and cried.

As he had promised, the man was back early next morning. The nurses were keeping George very busy. One nurse was taking his temperature; one was taking his blood pressure; one was giving him a pill ("To make you sleepy, George," she said), and one was getting ready to give him a shot.

"It's going to hurt, George," she said, "but only for a moment."

She took his arm, and George let out a scream.

"But the needle hasn't touched you yet," said the nurse, laughing. "There—now it's done. That wasn't so bad, was it?"
No, it really was not.
And anyway, it was
over now.

By the time the attendant came with the stretcher to wheel him to the operating room, George was getting sleepy. He tried hard to stay awake. He was curious to see what would happen next.

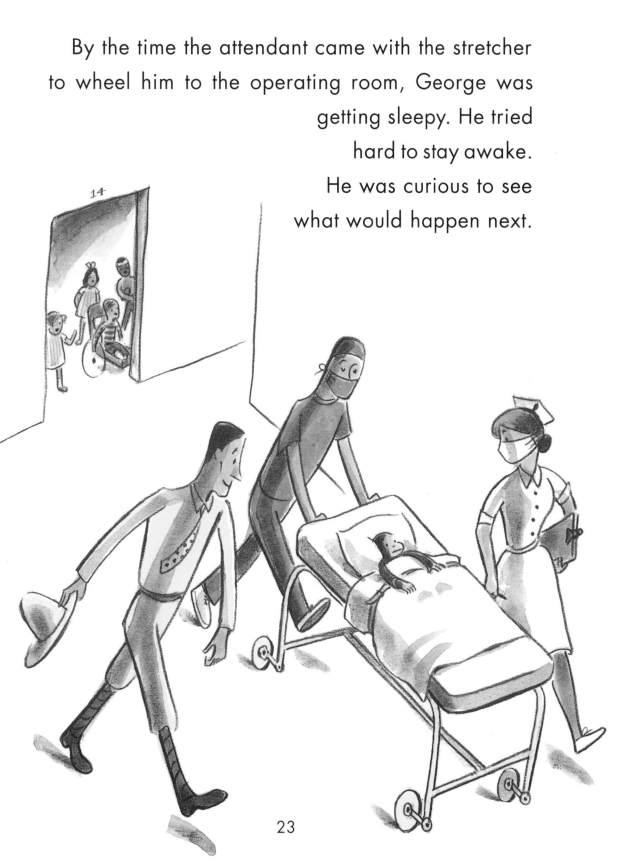

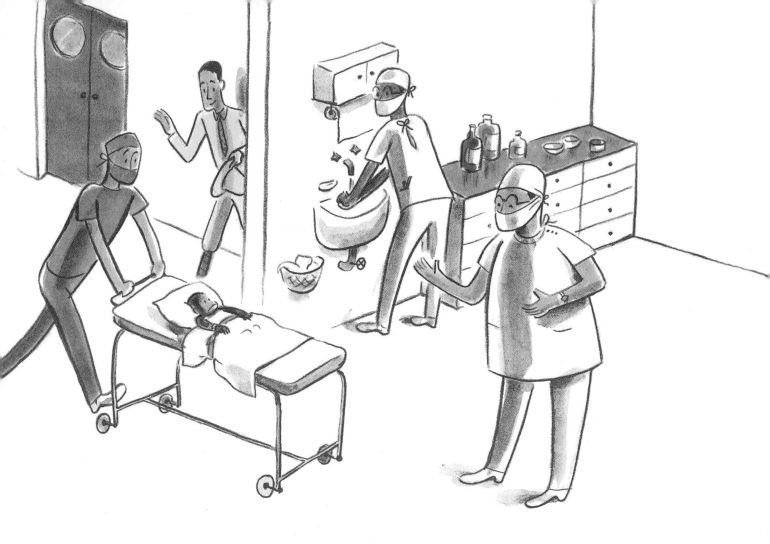

He could see a big table with bright lamps over it and doctors and nurses all around. They had caps on their heads and masks over their faces; only their eyes were showing.

One of the doctors winked at George and patted his head. It was Doctor Baker, who had

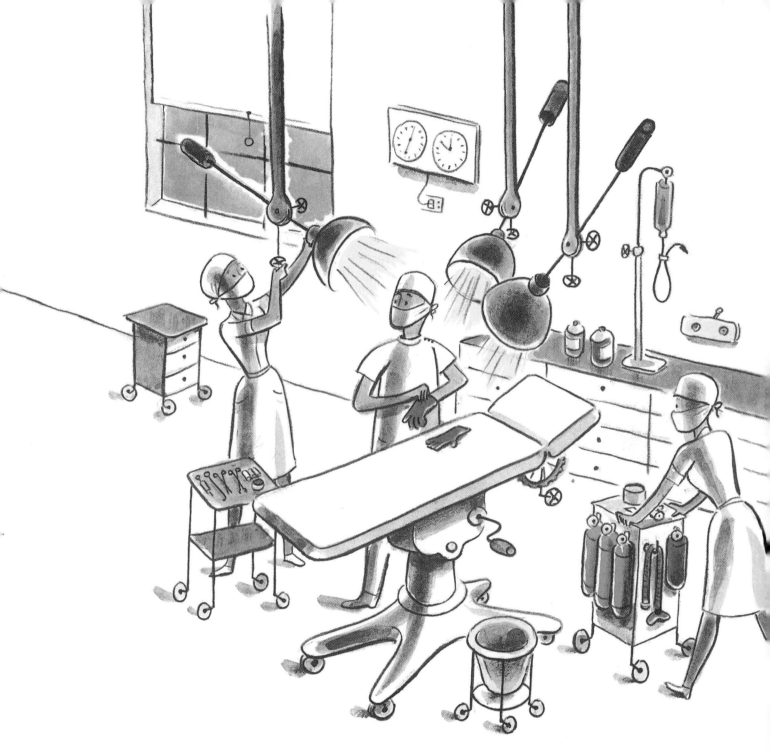

been to the house when it all had started. He looked funny with his mask on . . . And then George was fast asleep.

When George woke up he did not know what
had happened. He did not even know where he
was. Then he saw Nurse Carol. "It's all done,
George," she said. "They got the piece out. In a
day or two you will be running around again."

The man had brought him a picture book. But
George felt sick and dizzy. His throat was hurting,
too. He was not even curious about the new book.
He closed his eyes again. "We'll let him sleep,"
said Nurse Carol. "The more he sleeps, the better."

The next morning George felt better. He even ate a dish of ice cream. Dr. Baker came to see him, and the man, of course, came too.

Betsy was watching him from time to time. She seemed a little less sad, but she still did not smile.

Steve wheeled his go-cart over to George's bed. "Tomorrow I can get up and try to walk," he said. "Boy, I can hardly wait."

"I'll take you to the playroom now, George,"
Nurse Carol said the next morning, "and in the
afternoon your friend will come and take you
home."

The playroom was full of children. A lady was
showing Betsy how to use finger paint. There were
all sorts of things to play with, even a puppet
theater—and that was just the thing for George.
He had four hands so could handle four puppets
at the same time.

George gave
a real puppet show,
with a dragon
and a clown
and a bear
and a policeman.

The children laughed
and shouted,
and even Betsy
for the
first time
smiled a little.

29

There was a TV set in the playroom and also a record player. George was curious: If he climbed on the record player and turned the switch,

would it go round
and round like a
real merry-go-round?

It did!
It started slowly,
then it went faster and
faster, and whoopee!
George had lost his
balance and was
sailing through the air . . .

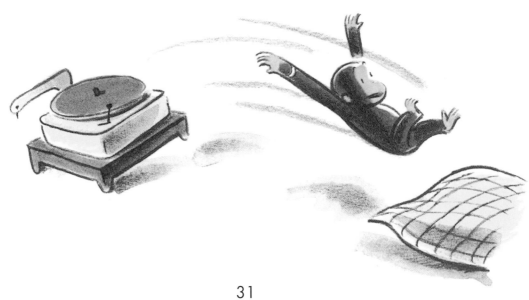

Luckily George landed on a soft cushion. The children cheered, and Betsy smiled again. George was SO funny.

But then the play lady picked George up. "That's enough for now," she said. "You'd better take a nap before lunch. We have a big day ahead of us. The mayor is coming to visit the hospital today, and later on you will be going home, George."

When George woke up,
Steve was just taking his first steps.
A nurse was helping him, and the children were
watching.

The go-cart was standing there empty.
George was curious.
He looked at it.
Then he climbed
into it.

Then he grabbed
the wheels and then, while
nobody was looking, he wheeled the go-cart right
out of the room.

George
could make
the go-cart go very fast.
This was fun! Down the hall he went.
By now the nurse had noticed that he
was gone and came running after him.
"George! George!" she shouted.

But George was
too excited to listen.
He wheeled around the corner
and down the ramp to the floor below,
where some men were busy pushing
lunch carts, and a lot of doctors and

nurses were showing the mayor around.

George tried to stop,
but it was too late.
WHAM!—the go-cart landed
right in the middle of everything.
Lunch carts tumbled. Spinach and scrambled
eggs and strawberry jam were all over the floor.
People fell over each other, and George was
thrown out of the go-cart and landed right in
the mayor's arms.

What a mess it was!

"You broke all my dishes!" someone cried.

"He ruined the go-cart!" complained another.

"What will the mayor think of it?" whispered someone else. And so it went.

Suddenly everybody looked up and listened.
From above came happy laughter—and there
stood Betsy, laughing, laughing, laughing. Then
the children joined in, then the mayor started
laughing, and finally everybody just laughed and
laughed. Everybody, that is, except George.

Betsy came running down the ramp, threw her arms around George, and kissed him. "Don't be sad, George," she said. "The whole thing was SO funny! I never laughed so much in my life. I'm so glad you were in the hospital with me."

Now the director of the hospital spoke: "I am sorry this happened, Mr. Mayor," he said, "but I think we'll just clean up the mess and be done with it."

"George," he went on, "you've made a terrible mess. But you also made our sad little Betsy happy again, and that is more than any of us has done.

"And now I see your friend has just come to take you home. So, goodbye, George, and take good care of yourself."

The children
crowded around the
windows waving goodbye when
George and the man with the yellow
hat were finally leaving the hospital.

44

As the car was
turning into the driveway
Nurse Carol came running after them. "Here's
a little package with something that belongs to
you, George," she called. "But don't open it before you are home!"

George was curious—
well, who would not be?
The moment he reached home
he ripped the paper off,
tore open the box—
and THERE

was the piece
of the puzzle
that had caused
all the trouble!

"How nice of the doctor to save it for us!" said the man with the yellow hat. "And NOW we can finish the puzzle."

The End

Dear Reader,

I first came to appreciate the compelling message of *Curious George Goes to the Hospital* as a young resident at the Boston Children's Hospital. Now, nearly fifty years later, this book continues to be read and loved by millions of children and their parents throughout the world. In celebration of this anniversary, I am honored to write this afterword.

While living in Cambridge, Massachusetts, Margret Rey formed a friendship and partnership with Myra Fox, the greatly respected head "play lady" (they are now called child life specialists) at Boston Children's Hospital. Myra asked the Reys to write a book that would help prepare children for a hospital experience. The result was *Curious George Goes to the Hospital*. An immediate success, the book was enthusiastically embraced by parents, nurses, child life specialists, and physicians.

Fifty years have passed since the book's publication. Much has changed: Single and double rooms, allowing for parents to sleep over with their child, have replaced hospital wards. Men and women serve as both nurses and as physicians (and nurses no longer wear those iconic caps!). Flexible endoscopes can remove a swallowed puzzle piece, making surgery unnecessary. And now, in what would delight George, clowns populate children's hospitals, giving cheer and happiness to parents, children, and even the staff.

But other essential elements of the vineyards of healing at children's hospitals gratefully remain: nurses on a daily basis exhibit empathy and deep caring for their young and very sick charges, skilled physicians apply the best of modern medicine to the illnesses affecting their patients, child life specialists bring happiness, excitement, and emotional support to their patients, and care workers from all medical disciplines rejoice when they send their young patients home cured and well.

For fifty years *Curious George Goes to the Hospital* has done its job very well. It has brought joy in the face of sadness, and humor to an experience that is often filled with fear.

So we all say, gratefully, happy anniversary, Curious George.

Frederick H. Lovejoy Jr., M.D.
ASSOCIATE PHYSICIAN IN CHIEF
BOSTON CHILDREN'S HOSPITAL

Here are some tips from Boston Children's Hospital:

BEFORE THE HOSPITAL

- Choose a quiet time to talk about the upcoming hospitalization.
- Reassure your child that the hospitalization, procedure,
  or test is the right thing to do.
- Use a calm and reassuring voice.
- Try not to make promises you can't keep. For example, don't tell your
  child that nothing is going to hurt.
- Encourage your child to ask you, doctors, and nurses lots of questions.

AT THE HOSPITAL

- As much as possible, follow the same rules and schedule
  that you use at home.
- Make your child's space personal.
  Bring family photos and your child's favorite pillow, blanket, or toy.
- Encourage your child to express his or her feelings and
  ask lots of questions.
- Plan something to look forward to every day, like a visit to the playroom
  or a special DVD.
- Plan time for family and friends to visit.
- Make time for yourself.